I Wonder About Allah (Book Two)

Published by
THE ISLAMIC FOUNDATION

Distributed by
KUBE PUBLISHING LTD
Tel :+44 (0)1530 249230, Fax: (0)1530 249656
E-mail: info@kubepublishing.com
Website: www.kubepublishing.com

First published in Turkey by Uğurböceği Publications, a Zafer Publication Group imprint, in 2008.

Text © 2014 Özkan Öze
Translation by Selma Aydüz
Illustrations © 2014 Zafer Publishing

Author Özkan Öze
Translator Selma Aydüz
Series editor Dr Salim Aydüz
Illustrator Sevgi İçigen
Book design Zafer Publishing & Nasir Cadir
Cover design Fatima Jamadar

A Cataloguing-in-Publication Data record for this book is available from the British Library

ISBN 978-0-86037-503-6
eISBN 978-0-86037-548-7

Printed by Imak Ofset, Turkey

BOOK

I WONDER ABOUT ALLAH

Özkan Öze

Translated by Selma Aydüz
Illustrations: Sevgi İçigen

Contents

Foreword

THE STORY OF the "I Wonder About Islam" series started one day with my son asking me, "Why can't I see Allah, dad?" He asked this question at such an unexpected time that I didn't know what answer to give him.

I actually knew the answer. But when he asked so suddenly, I just said, "Umm, well…" He opened his eyes wide and started staring at me as if to say *Come on, give me the answer!* I beat around the bush for a while. You know, I was humming and hawing. In the end, I said, "Your eyes are so small, yet Allah is so big! This is the answer to the question. Because of this, you can't see Allah!"

"Oh, really?" he said. He turned his Spider-Man toy around in his hands. Then, as if he hadn't said anything, he went to his room. He was only five years old…

Perhaps, for a child his age, this answer was

enough. At the time, I had handled the situation. However, as he got older, he would ask heaps of new questions about Allah. In that case, I had to start preparing straight away.

So, that is how I started the "I Wonder About Islam" series.

The best thing about this book is that not only my kids, but kids from around the world can read my answers.

The "I Wonder About Islam" series' first and second books consist of answers I have given to questions about Allah.

In the third book, you will find answers to questions about the Prophet, peace be upon him.

The fourth book is about the Muslim holy book, The Qur'an.

As for the fifth book, the topic is death and life after death. In particular, you will find answers to questions you have about heaven.

In the sixth book, I brought together answers to questions about belief in fate.

The last book of the series is about angels.

Have I answered all the questions about all these topics? Of course not!

I only tried to answer the most frequently asked ones. But the questions I gave answers to will enlighten you in terms of the questions I didn't manage to answer as well.

My aim from the start wasn't to answer all questions; it was so that when a question comes to mind, you have the correct logic and viewpoint to approach it.

I think we largely achieved this. After reading this book, you will see that questions don't frighten you as much as before.

You will bravely ask the questions you thought were the hardest to answer, and soon you will see that you can't think of a question that doesn't have an answer.

You should never be afraid of asking questions, and don't ever give up asking questions! Because a question is a key. Every question opens a door for you. And behind every door is a whole other world.

Hang on to the question's tail and pull as much as you can. A huge answer will follow it.

Furthermore, asking a question is also a prayer.

Asking a question is saying, "I want to learn!",

"I want to understand!", "I want to know better and love more!"

Make sure you do these types of prayers a lot so that your mind and heart is filled with the light of knowledge; so that your path is always bright.

The "I Wonder About Islam" series have been written using the works of the great Muslim scholar Said Nursi (1878–1960). The answers given to the questions and the examples to help you understand the topics have all been taken from his *Risale-i Nur* books.

Özkan Öze
İstanbul, 2012

Why did Allah create the universe?

It was not without purpose that We created the heavens and the earth and everything in between.
Surah Sad 38:27

YOU MAY BE a great artist. On the paper that your brush touches, flowers trees and all sorts of landscapes turn into a painting.

But we won't be able to know of your artistic talent without seeing any of your work.

You will be the only one who knows of your own ability, your skill, and your talent!

If you want others to see it, you must make a painting and show it to other people. You migh open a gallery. You might invite people to the gallery.

People would then come and see your amazing work.

In this way, we would have all seen and understood what a great artist you are.

We would appreciate you, and gaze at your work with amazement.

We would investigate your skill, look at how you drew a tree, what colours you painted the flowers, how you could make the horses so noble and make rabbits so cute with a few lines.

If you want to be known and recognised, if you say others should see the beauty of your art and your precious work, then you must make artwork and exhibit them in galleries.

Otherwise, none of us would know how the papers your brush touches turn into a painting. If you don't show us your art, then your skill, your ability and your talent would remain unknown to us.

We would leave this world without knowing and loving your art.

So, in this way, if Allah hadn't created the universe, we would never get to know Him. Because just like everything else in the universe, we also would not have been created.

Only Allah would have known what kind of a Creator He is. Because there would have been nothing else, only Allah.

There was only Allah...

Before the universe was created there was only Allah. But Allah could still create anything.

But only He knew this.

Allah's might was endless before He created more stars in the sky than sand particles on Earth.

But only He knew this.

Allah was the Giver of Life before He chose the Earth from countless planets in the sky to cover with an atmosphere and seas on its surface, then adorned it with streams and mountains, made plants, animals and humans.

But only He knew this.

Before He decorated the Earth's fields, vineyards and gardens with a thousand different sorts of flowers...

Before He painted these flowers with a

number of different colours…

Before He gave roses a smell and daisies a golden heart…

Allah was the Creator of everything.

But only He knew this.

Not only did Allah have the power to create and give life, He was also very compassionate to every being He created.

He was the One who knew everything when there was nothing.

He heard all voices and conversations.

He saw all things in both darkness and light, both near and far.

He could resurrect the dead.

His generosity and kindness was limitless.

He could give faith to hearts.

But He was the only One who knew all this.

And our Lord wished to be known. He created the universe to show all this beauty.

See, this universe is like a huge gallery that shows Allah's countless qualities and endless abilities.

In it we'll see His workmanship's grace and brilliance on every kind of canvas.

The blue sky is a canvas.

The starry night is a canvas.

Butterfly wings are a canvas.

Fruitful trees are a canvas.

And babies sucking from their mothers' breasts are a whole other canvas; it shows us how our Lord's infinite compassion shines on each baby.

As we open our eyes and look, we see His masterpieces all around us.

Some of us say MASHALLAH, as God has willed.

"Mashallah! Allah wished to create these butterflies so beautiful, so pleasant and so colourful"

Some of us say SUBHANALLAH, glory be to God.

"Subhanallah! Allah, who created this blue sky, decorated it with these white clouds and created this rainbow that brings happiness to those who see it, is far from any defect and fault!"

Some of us say ALLAHU AKBAR, God is great.

"Allahu Akbar! The One who decorates the night's face with billions of stars is great!

"The One who makes each star swim in the seas of the sky is great!

"The One who hangs one of those stars, the Sun, as a lamp for us and the Moon as a lantern for our nights is great!"

Did Allah need to create the universe?

*Allah, Who is in need of none and
of Whom all are in need*
Surah al-Ikhlas 112:2

I THOUGHT A question like this would come to your mind because many things in our world are made to meet some of our needs.

Before I answer this question, let me first give you an example. A man who opens a stall to sell lemons does this to earn money. Because he needs money. Actually, he needs countless things that he can buy with the money: salt, bread, water, soap, a house, shoes and so on.

If one day he inherited a large amount of money from an unexpected place, he wouldn't sell lemons anymore. Because he wouldn't need money anymore.

If you saw him still going from place to place, selling lemons from his stall, you would know he didn't do his job for the money.

The man continues to sell lemons because he likes to and wants to sell lemons. Not because he needs to.

If you saw that he even gave lemons for free to those who don't have money, or even that he doesn't take money from anyone, you will be convinced that this man doesn't do this job for another reason.

If they asked him, "What need do you have to sell lemons?"

He would say, "I'm not selling lemons because I need to! I don't need the money that is given for the lemons!

"I like selling lemons. It pleases me to offer lemons to people."

The man does this job because he wants to, because he is generous, because he enjoys giving out lemons and making people happy.

If he didn't do it, nothing would be lost. No one would say, "Why don't you give out lemons to us?"

Because he has no obligation to do it!

Therefore, even in the world full of our endless needs, sometimes people do things, good deeds, acts of charity, without asking for anything in return or a profit.

Rich and generous people feed the hungry, clothe the poor. They have no obligation to do so; they could or could not do it.

No one would ask, "What need did you have? You fed us, you held these feasts, why?" It would be rude and ungrateful if they did.

Let's look at our question now through the window of this example.

"Did Allah need to create the universe?"

Allah is As-Samad

One of Allah's beautiful names is As-Samad. As-Samad means, He who has no need of anything else, yet everything else has the need of Him.

Allah does not need this universe, nor did He need to create this universe, or need anything else.

Allah was there when this whole universe wasn't. He who was there when nothing else was, does not need anything!

Would Allah, who was there when the Sun wasn't, need the Sun? Or need the Moon?

Would he need the earth, air, water or soil?

What would Allah need from trees?

What good would birds flying or clouds floating past bring to Allah?

Allah didn't create all these for a need. He created because He wanted to.

As I explained to you in the previous chapter, He created to show His unique workmanship.

He could have created or not created.

Allah doesn't need anything.

But Allah chose to create, to bring into existence, to show us His workmanship and introduce Himself to us.

Because of this, we could taste the blessing of being alive.

We saw this beautiful, magnificent universe

full of wonders and curiosities.

We heard sounds. We kissed a baby on its cheek. We touched a rose petal, took in the beautiful scent of it.

We experienced a mother's love, felt a father's compassion.

We found out how sweet honey is, how delicious milk is.

We found out the differences between the seasons.

We discovered how every snowflake is different from every other.

We watched with amazement how apples

were created on branches.

We watched birds flying, bees collecting honey.

We ran, walked, lay down and slept.

We loved, were loved, got excited, became happy.

When we got scared, we took refuge with Allah and read prayers. We thanked Allah for creating us and letting us know of Him.

We said, "I am here!"

We said, "I have a Lord!"

Neither more nor less!

Just think of the Sun! It reflects on all things on Earth. On every particle of dew on a flower, on rivers flowing pleasantly, on the windows of houses, on every piece of glass furniture and all mirrors, the Sun reflects and shimmers. It appears on them with its light and heat like a mini-sun. Well, does this have any benefit to the Sun?

No!

What if the Sun didn't reflect on anything?

Would it get any smaller if it didn't shine on a molecule? Would there be any reduction in its heat and light?

No!

If the sun didn't send light and heat to the Earth, the Earth, not the Sun, would lose from this. The Sun would still be the Sun but the Earth would be cold and in pitch-black darkness.

Like the Sun, our Lord's endless skill and might shone on the Earth.

So all stars, suns, moons…

All flowers smiling on the Earth…

Ears of wheat, all sprouting seeds…

Seeing eyes, hearing ears, speaking tongues, beating hearts…

Clouds, rain droplets, snowflakes…

These are all little shimmers of Allah's infinite ability.

Allah doesn't need any of them. Neither his skill nor might increase or decrease because He created the universe.

Allah didn't create the universe because He needed it; He created because He wanted to.

"When We will something to happen, all that We say is, 'Be,' and it is."

Surah al-Nahl 16:40

Everything is for us

While Allah isn't dependent on anything, we need everything in this universe.

The Sun brightens our day with its light, the Moon is a lantern to our nights.

The rain waters our gardens.

Forests work night and day to clean the air we breathe. Countless leaves on countless branches of countless trees work like a factory to increase the oxygen in the air.

And we need all of these things.

We are the servants who need everything from Allah, Who doesn't need anything.

This universe works for us. Without it we would not have been able to exist.

While the cows work like a milk factory, bees serve up sweet honey.

Chickens lay eggs in perfectly packaged shells.

Mountains' mines contain rocks and minerals for our countless needs.

We need all of these things in the universe, and so much more, to survive.

We are the servants who need everything from Allah, Who doesn't need anything.

Why did Allah create humans?

MY FIVE YEAR old son asked me the other day, "Why did Allah make me a human?" As the word "created" hadn't exactly found meaning in his world yet, he chose to use the word "make".

I needed to give a quick answer so I said, "Since the best being is a human, Allah made you the best being!"

He didn't get it! "Why?"

"As a human is the best being and as Allah likes you, He wanted you to be a human and created you as a human!"

"Are humans the best?"

"Of course, or would you prefer to be a frog?"

"I wouldn't!"

"An octopus?"

"I wouldn't!"

"A spider?"

"Hmm! Could it be both a spider and a man?"

He wanted to say, "Can it be Spider-Man!" but he couldn't say it bluntly. If I said, "It could, it could!" he would then ask, "Why didn't Allah make me a Spider-Man?"

Instead, I was able to say, "No way! What you said would only happen in films. Choose one, a spider or a man."

"A man of course! It's best to be a man!"

And Allah created man

The Sun was just another star amongst billions, in a galaxy amongst a billion other galaxies that Allah had created.

It wasn't so different from other stars. It's

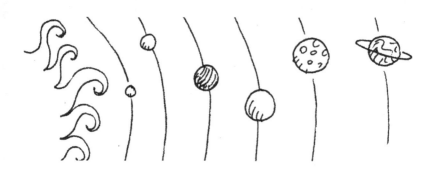

not very large, for example.

However, its fate was much brighter than its star siblings. Because surrounding it was our little world amongst eight other planets.

The Sun had been given the job of a lamp that brightens the Earth's days.

Allah put such a carefully calculated distance between the Sun and the Earth that those planets closer than it get scorched surfaces from the hundreds of degrees of heat, whereas those further away than the Earth are cold and dark.

The Earth's uniqueness is not just due to this.

Mountains and deep valleys have been carved in it.

Rocks have been turned to soil and the bottom of the sea has been covered in a soft sand.

The little Earth's surface was wrapped with a blue atmosphere. In this blue atmosphere, clouds as big as mountains were created and rain started falling onto the earth in droplets.

Rivers, brooks and streams started flowing from the slopes of mountains.

Sweet fountains were created, squirting through stones and rocks.

Seas were filled, overflowed, waves started greeting the rocks.

In this state, the Earth was very different from all other planets and stars. But like them it was still dead, as there was no trace of life or spirit.

And then Allah created life on Earth.

Life started to flow from all parts of the Earth.

Life, which didn't exist in soil, rocks, water or the Sun, was created on Earth.

Fields were furnished with green grass.

Colourful and sweet-smelling flowers bloomed on Earth; trees started to grow millimetre by millimetre.

Forests filled the slopes of mountains.

The Earth was alive and rejoiced!

But this wasn't all.

Allah created animals.

He created honeybees flying in between those colourful flowers, birds tweeting and chirping on tree branches in the morning.

He created finches, sparrows and nightingales.

He created antelopes with beautiful eyes, lions in savannahs.

He created brave horses whose hoof beats echo in deserted valleys.

He created dolphins, giant whales, tiny

horse mackerels and limpets with their shells in curls.

Oysters growing pearls on their lap and colourful corals and squids and octopus and starfish.

He created sheep bleating in meadows.

He created cows that walk while shaking their heads from side to side eating fresh grass.

So now the Earth had come to a state that was nothing like any other planet in space.

Even the Moon, which stays right next to the Earth and shines like a bright lamp, didn't possess any of the life on Earth.

The Earth was like an amazing painting. But it wasn't complete yet.

And then Allah created humans!

Being human is special

Allah created man! And He gave man some characteristics that He didn't give to any other being.

For example, the eye Allah gave to humans is very different to a cow's eye!

No! I'm not talking about the eye's sizes, shape or colour! I'm talking about how the eye sees!

For a cow that grazes from morning to evening in meadows, a blood red poppy is no different from a tasteless plant.

Maybe the cow's eye sees the poppy but doesn't see the beauty in it.

No cow can think, *How that bright red poppy suits that green grass! Allah created this poppy so beautifully!*

The cow's huge eyes don't *see* that beauty…

Only a human eye can *see* it.

The ears Allah gave to humans are also very different from the ones He gave to donkeys.

No! Of course I'm not talking about the height and shape difference between human and donkey ears. Everyone knows that anyway.

Of course, a donkey's ears also hear a nightingale's voice trilling on an old willow branch. It would hear it, but no donkey on Earth would be mesmerised enough by that nightingale's magical song to think, *Allah taught these birds such beautiful songs, gave them such beautiful voices!*

Because although a donkey's ears hear the nightingale's voice, they don't *hear* the beauty in it...

Only a human ear can *hear* it.

No human's nose can smell as well as a dog's nose. But no dog has ever *smelled* a rose.

A dog wouldn't be carried away by a rose's smell. No dog would think, *Allah created these roses so beautifully and on top of that added such a smell!*

Even if a dog takes in a rose's smell, it won't take in the beauty of it.

Only a human nose will.

Allah gave bears a mouth and a tongue that tastes and a stomach that gets hungry.

Bears eat pears and so do humans. They

even say bears eat the best pears.

Therefore bears, just like humans, taste the pears.

But no bear would think, *Mashallah, this pear tastes so nice and smells so nice. Allah creates such beautiful fruits from the branches of trees that drink nothing but muddy water through their roots. The taste is so nice; the smell is also so nice!*

Even if the bear's tongue tastes the pears, it won't get the true *taste* behind it.

Only a human tongue will enjoy the *taste* of knowing Allah, Who offers these beautiful fruits to us through the hands of tree branches.

A human's eye has been created different from a cow's eye.

A human's ears different from a donkey's.

A human's nose different from a dog's.

And a human's tongue different from a bear's.

A human will *see* what they can't see, *hear* what they can't hear, *smell* what they can't smell and *taste* whate they can't taste.

And in front of all the beautiful things they see, hear, smell and taste they will be able to do what other beings, from ants to elephants can't do: they will think *Our Lord created everything so beautifully!*

They will say, "His might and workmanship is so great!"

They will say, "Thanks to our Lord, who surrounds us with these blessings!"

Humans, who know and recognise Allah in this way, also obey messengers chosen from amongst them.

They take notice of these messengers' words.

They also have faith in holy words brought down from their Lord through messengers.

They stay away from things Allah forbids them.

They also do things Allah commands them to do…

They pray, they mention their Lord's name a lot.

So Allah both loves these servants and also rewards them for not staying blind, deaf, emotionless and silent to the creation of this magnificent Earth and carrying out the task given to them.

He takes them from here to a far more beautiful and amazing place.

Those who think of Allah when they are eating a delicious fruit here are rewarded with delicious fruit eternally.

Those who think of their Lord when they

see a beautiful flower here are rewarded by living in gardens full of beautiful flowers for eternity.

Those who think of Allah's greatness frequently here, are greeted with blessings that suit His greatness there.

And there they live in happiness forever.

but We shall admit those who believe and do good deeds into Gardens graced with flowing streams, there to remain for ever – a true promise from God. Who speaks more truly than God?

Surah Al-Nisa' 4:122

Why does Allah create some people 'ugly'?

DO YOU LIKE TURNIPS? To this day, I have never eaten one but I know that, if I tasted it, I wouldn't like it. Of course, like all food Allah has created, a turnip is good and beneficial and looking down on it and bad mouthing it is shameful.

I wouldn't do such a thing. But I can't eat a turnip. What can I do? I have no appetite for it!

My tongue doesn't get excited about the taste, neither does my nose for the smell.

However, I have this friend. He is a turnip monster.

Turnip, which makes me feel sick, is as delicious as cake or pizza for him.

Turnips, in which I don't see any beauty in terms of its taste and smell, is the best of all vegetables for him! Strange, so strange!

Now if I said, "Allah created cucumbers so delicious and beautiful, but why did He create this poor turnip so ugly and revolting?" wouldn't my turnip loving friend say, "Where do you get that idea? Turnips are as delicious and beautiful as cucumbers! Besides there are vitamins in tunips that are good for you."

Then I would understand that a turnip isn't ugly at all! Only I can't see the beauty in it!

A man on the ferry

One day I saw a man on the ferry crossing the Bosphorus river, in Istanbul. He seemed so ugly to me that – forgive me Allah – I thought to myself, *Allah, why did You create this man so ugly?* Then I felt very guilty. I asked God for forgiveness for belittling one of His servants.

After some time, a woman and a child with a huge bagel in his hand came and sat next to the man. The woman was this man's wife. She had gone to the bottom floor of the ferry to buy a bagel for the little child.

As soon as the man saw the boy, he smiled a huge smile. And the child returned a smile to his father that was unexpectedly big from his little face.

The man asked, "Did you get your bagel, my little one?"

The child happily showed the bagel to his dad.

The man said, "Break a little bit off and let me taste it."

The kid handed over his bagel.

The man proudly said to his wife, "My generous son, look he's giving it all!" Then he picked up his son and they hugged, with bagel covered hands, in such a way that you would think they hadn't see each other for years.

Then his dad kissed the son on his cheeks. The kid started to kiss him back.

"Come on: kissing race!" said the man.

Then they started to have a 'who can kiss first race' with the kid. Sometimes the man

won, other times the child.

The ferry was filled with the sounds of this father and son kissing.

As for the mother, she watched the love of her husband and son with watery eyes; just like me and all of the other passengers on the ferry.

I looked at them and, rather than the ugly man I had seen before, I saw the world's sweetest dad sitting there. My insides filled with the fire of guilt once again due to the thoughts that crossed my mind before.

"Allah," I said, "you create such beautiful servants!"

You must have immediately understood the similarity between my attitude towards turnips and my attitude towards the man on the ferry. They were both shallow and silly. In reality, neither the turnip nor the man were ugly!

The turnip possesses a special taste and is full of vitamins. As for the man, I didn't think he was good looking but he was a good man. And in the eyes of the child, he was the best father in the world.

You were asking, "Why did Allah create some people ugly?" Right?

Did you manage to get a bit of an answer?

Allah doesn't actually create anyone ugly. He gives people different kinds of beauty.

Beautiful for some, ugly for others; ugly for some, beautiful for others

What's beautiful to one person, seems ugly to another. What's ugly to one, seems beautiful to another.

I know you like stories so listen to this:

A long time ago some people told their Sultan about a man named Majnun. "Oh Sultan, this man they call Majnun is about to die of his love. He wanders around in the desert. He says 'Leila' and nothing else. He kisses dogs just because they come from the city Leila lives in!"

The Sultan became very curious about the beauty of this Leila that made Majnun fall in love in such a way. He ordered, "Bring me this Leila! Let's see what she's like!"

The Sultan's men found Leila. But they didn't stop there and brought Majnun to the palace as well.

The Sultan looked at Majnun first.

Poor Majnun was in a terrible state.

Then he turned and looked at Leila. And what should he see?

Majnun's Leila was a fair and weak girl. What's more she had a face full of freckles! The Sultan didn't think Leila was beautiful at all.

He asked Majnun, "Is this the girl that brought you to this state of love?"

Majnun lifted his head, smiled and replied to the Sultan, "Oh Sultan! If you could only see her through my eyes!"

In this story, you can see how terms such as 'beauty' change from person to person. The Sultan turned up his nose at Leila, but Majnun wandered the deserts looking for her.

Leila, whom the Sultan found ugly, was the world's most beautiful thing for Majnun.

Now you tell me, did Allah create Leila beautiful or ugly?

Should we believe the Sultan or Majnun?

I don't believe either of them. I don't listen to either of their words. Because Leila can't be ugly because the Sultan finds her ugly; or be beautiful because Majnun finds her beautiful.

I know you're confused. You can't decide whether Leila is ugly or beautiful anyway.

You can't decide who's really beautiful and really ugly with measures that change so much.

This is why you need a measure that doesn't change from person to person, from eye to eye, from heart to heart, from time to time.

Beauty is what's left in your hands

Wearing a beautiful dress can make us seem beautiful. But when we take off that dress and put it in a cupboard, the beauty it gave to us will be gone too. Therefore, the beauty the dress gives is temporary, it doesn't belong to us.

When the dress is gone, the beauty is also gone.

An ugly dress, then, can make us look ugly. But it wouldn't make us truly ugly. When we take off the dress, there would be nothing left of the ugliness.

Our body is like a dress for us. Other people may think it is beautiful or ugly. This dress will

get old one day and it's a dress that one day we will leave under the soil.

What makes us is our mind, soul, conscience, heart, dreams, hopes, beliefs, fears, joys, and other similar things under our body.

And just as a beautiful dress can't make someone truly beautiful, a body beautiful on the surface doesn't make someone truly beautiful.

An ugly body doesn't make anyone ugly either.

And whether they are ugly or beautiful, everyone will leave this world; and when they leave, they will take off the dress of the body that they'd been wearing and leave it behind.

And what's left in their hands will be:
- their good and bad deeds;
- their fairness or cruelty;
- generosity or greediness;
- worship or rebellion;
- belief or non-belief;
- merits and sins.

In other words, their true beauty; or true ugliness.

Then it will be clear who is truly beautiful, and who is truly ugly.

Appearances are deceiving

There was a man named Zahir ibn Haram, who loved the Prophet, peace be upon him, a lot. He lived in the desert. He was a bit ugly. When he went to Madinah, he brought the Prophet presents.

And the Prophet gave him a variety of

things he needed and made him happy.

One day the Prophet saw him in the market place. He quietly crept up on him and covered his eyes while hugging him and said, "Who would like to buy this slave?"

The man recognised that the one holding him was the Prophet from his voice. He said, "Oh Allah's Messenger! What would anyone do with an ugly slave like me? You won't earn much by selling me!"

The Prophet, peace be upon him, complimented him and pleased his heart by saying to him, "Those who are deceived by appearances maybe wouldn't give much for you, but your worth is a lot with Allah!"

Why does Allah make some people disabled or ill?

I HAD A friend, let's pretend his name was Mustafa. We used to see each other a lot. After we started living in different cities, we couldn't see each other that much. When you asked me this question, he was the first person that came to mind.

I called him. We talked for a bit, he was fine. He was working in a telephone company.

He had got married. He had recently had a son.

"My son," he said, "runs around the house so much I can't catch up with him!" We both laughed at this a lot!

Do you know why I thought of him? Because he had a car accident six years ago.

They had to amputate his right leg below his knee.

At first, he found it really hard. Even though he had a strong belief in Allah, he kept asking, "Why me? Why did this accident happen to me?"

His protests increased each day due to the people around him.

His relatives and a few bone-headed friends kept saying things to him like, "What a pity! Such a young man left disabled! This is a terrible fate!"

I couldn't understand this.

But it didn't seem like he would listen to me if I talked to him face-to-face. So, I sat and wrote him a letter.

I still keep a copy of that letter. It may be useful for you to read what I wrote.

Dear Mustafa

Of course, just like everyone else, I'm upset about the accident that happened to you. I felt sorrowful; I prayed for you, I asked for well-being and patience for you from Allah.

But I'll tell you now, I'm not going to say "what a pity" like those people around you and feel sorry for you.

No, I'm not going to do that. If you're expecting something like that from me, don't bother reading this letter!

Of course, I don't know what it's like to lose a foot. But no matter what situation you are in I can't understand people saying, "Why did this accident happen to me? When there are so many people in the world, why did Allah choose me for this trial? What did I do wrong to deserve this disability?"

Dear Mustafa, listen to my words. If you continue to question why this happened to you, you will never be able to get out from underneath that upside down car.

When the sky is so large and the sun is so bright, you shouldn't let a single dark cloud block the light from your life.

The tailor and his model

Once upon a time, there was a tailor. He was quite an expert tailor. His reputation and the fame of the clothes he made had spread throughout the whole world.

This expert tailor hired this poor and lonely man to model the outfits he sewed.

He dressed the man in different clothes, each item more beautiful than the one before it, and saw how they looked. He cut left and right in his own way, sliced and sewed.

One day that poor and lonely man said to the expert tailor, "Why are you cutting up this suit you made me wear?

"It was just right for me. Don't you see how good it makes me look?"

The expert tailor replied to the man he'd been paying to be a model in this way, "What right do you have to say such things to me? The suit you are wearing is not your property! I made you wear it for a certain purpose.

"Now I'm cutting it up because of a number of reasons you don't know. I'm extending it or shortening it. I'm sewing wherever I need to.

"Have you forgotten your days of poverty and, instead of being thankful for this humble job, you're finding fault with me?"

So our story ends here.

This is a story that I really love. I haven't forgotten it since the day I read it. From time to time, I recall it, and at times I reread it. Especially, when I encounter some distressing events, remembering this little story has been a guiding light for me.

Now, think of your own body.

When you opened your eyes to the world, you were born with a human shape.

You hadn't earned this in any way.

You didn't pay a price to avoid being a sheep waiting its turn to be killed in a slaughterhouse.

Allah created you from nothing. He didn't make you a lifeless thing like a stone or a rock.

He didn't make you a plant like parsley, a turnip or a pear tree, either.

He also didn't make you a polar bear or a chestnut worm.

Yet at one time, neither you nor they existed!

There was no difference between Allah creating you or any of the things I mentioned.

There was only His wish. And Allah wished for you.

He created you in the best manner.

Don't you ever think of the times when you were nothing, the times when you looked like a chewed piece of meat in your mother's tummy?

Have you forgotten how your Lord changed you from state to state since that day and brought you into being. But due to this discomfort now, you complain, "Why me? Why did this accident happen to me?"

Are you going to push aside all the kindness of Allah, all the blessings because this accident happened to you?

Because He took back the foot He gave to you, are you going to rebel against Him with the tongue He gave, the mind He gave, the Heart He gave, the life He gave?

Be patient! If you are patient today, you will be very thankful tomorrow.

Mustafa, my dear friend, when you were born, you were born with a human shape, not a sheep's fur.

Would you take this shape off if it were possible?

Would you prefer to be a cat that always falls on four healthy feet rather than being a human with a crippled foot?

I can almost hear you say, "Are you mocking me?"

What if your eyes didn't see?

Your hands didn't feel!

Your ears didn't hear!

Would you then give up being a human?

Whatever the circumstances, you wouldn't want to leave your humanity and take on the shape of an animal, right?

My friend, I'm trying to explain to you that even though your foot may have gone, what's left in your hands is very precious.

If you don't realise this now, nothing will help. Even if you were as healthy as an athlete lifting weights at the Olympics, this still wouldn't be enough to make you happy.

Endless good news to you!

If we were to live on this Earth forever, your foot being amputated would be a disaster. Then I would feel as sorry for you as I could.

But as you know, the life on Earth is not infinite. Infinite life is the hereafter waiting for us after we die.

We will all leave this place one day. After our soul leaves it (old or young, we can't know), our most beloved will leave our bodies in the soil like a seed.

And when the time comes like our Lord promised us, we will be resurrected and sent to our real homes.

Your left foot started this journey a little earlier than you, that's all.

But don't worry!

In that infinite life, both your feet will be safe and sound.

The same good news goes for blind people. They will see in Heaven with more clarity than people do on Earth. For eternity as well.

Allah has prepared huge surprises in the hereafter for those like you suffering from various difficulties on Earth.

I want to finish my letter with two hadiths from the Prophet, peace be upon him. I hope what I wrote has lessened your pain.

See you soon.

"On the Day of Resurrection, when people who had suffered affliction are given their reward, those who were healthy will wish their skins had been cut to pieces with scissors when they were in the world."

— Tirmidhi

"Allah said, 'If I deprive my slave of his two beloved things (his eyes) and he remains patient, I will let him enter Paradise in compensation for them'."

— Bukhari

The woman with epilepsy

During the era of bliss, there was a woman with epilepsy. One day she came before the Prophet, peace be upon him, and made this request, "Oh, Allah's Messenger, I am an epilepsy patient. Could you pray for me so I recover from this illness?"

The Prophet said to the ill woman, "If you want I'll pray for you and you'll recover from

your illness. If you want you can be patient and get Heaven in return!"

The old woman replied in an appropriate way for a women of that era of bliss, "Oh Allah's Messenger! Since the reward of patience is so huge, I choose to be patient. But when I get a fit, I pull off my clothes. Please pray so that I don't pull off my clothes."

Then the Prophet prayed for her in this way. Allah always accepted his prayers.

How will Allah resurrect us after we die?

"Look, then at the imprints of God's mercy, how He restores the earth to life after death: this same God is the one who will return people to life after death – He has power over all things."
Surah al-Rum 30:50

IT WAS A day during the era of bliss. One of the Prophet's friends asked Allah's Messenger, peace be upon him, this question, "Oh Allah's Messenger! How does Allah resurrect all humans? Is there an example of this?"

The Prophet, peace be upon him, said, "Have you ever passed a valley where a tribe lives during a dry season? And then passed when it was green all around?"

The one asking the question replied, "Of course I did, Oh Allah's Messenger!"

Then the Prophet, peace be upon him, said, "This is proof of how Allah resurrects. Allah resurrects the dead in this way!"

The season is now spring

Only a few weeks ago the tree's branches were bare.

They looked sorrowful and lonely in front of the grey winter clouds, like skeletons. Old and carefree crows would settle on their branches.

Wherever you looked were quiet and colourless gardens.

No leaf, no flower, no fruit to see.

No birds chirping, no insect's buzz to hear, not even the silent flapping of a butterfly's wing.

Whatever happened, happened in a few weeks!

First, I saw a plum tree.

It was decorated from head to toe with white flowers. What joy, what glee, what life filled those dry branches.

"The plum tree," I said, "came back to life."

Then one sweet cool morning, a peach tree, wore a pink dress that brought happiness to a person.

"The peach tree," I said, "came back to life."

Grass on hills and billions of seeds in gardens started sprouting.

Flowers in pots and bees in hives woke up.

The dead dry earth found life again!

I realised, it was now the season of spring.

And there couldn't be a better time than this to give you an answer.

Because during every spring season, our Lord shows us billions of little examples of resurrection after death.

Every seed that splits, every dry branch that gets covered in flowers, every flower that wakes up answers your question:

"This is how you will be resurrected!

"This is how your Lord will bring you back to life!

"This easy, this fast!"

"He brings the living out of the dead and the dead out of the living. He gives life to the earth

after death, and you will be brought out in the same way."

Surah al-Rum 30:19

Which is easier?

Which is really easier: to do something for the first time, or the second time?

For example, if you lost your English homework or if you spilled water on it, would writing it again be as hard as writing it the first time?

Of course, it wouldn't.

Because you would pretty much have remembered the sentences you wrote before and it wouldn't be as hard to use the same sentences as it was to write them the first time.

If an artist made a painting, and then that painting got burnt to ashes, and the same artist said, "I'll do the painting again!" you can't say to him, "Come on, how are you going to do that? The painting turned to ashes, the wind blew the ashes away," because the one who did it the first time, will do it much easier the second time!

Allah created us from nothing once. He brought together our bodies atom by atom, cell by cell from water, air, soil, plants, all the food we eat whether dead or alive, and gave us this life.

Of course, there's no such thing as easy or hard for Allah. But for our mind to really understand resurrection after death we could say this: Our Lord who once creates from nothing, can of course create again after death if He wants. For His might, this is much easier than creating the first time.

Think of the people living two to three centuries ago. Now, none of them exist. The particles that made up their bodies have mixed up with the earth.

One day, like all living things, when we leave this world, whether the cells and atoms making up our bodies mix with soil, water and air or go into different plants and a variety of animal's bodies or spread to the four corners of the world, Allah, who collected us from such

messy places and created us the first time, will
create again!

Like He created billions of dead flowers
again in one spring…

Like He gave life again to millions of dry
branches…

And like all the seeds that were lying under
the soil, and suddenly came to life on a spring
day.

Rotten bones

It was the first years of Islam. The polytheists of Makkah had gathered and were talking amongst themselves. Ubayy ibn Khalaf, who was one of the ones who denied the Prophet's message the most, was amongst them.

He went to the Prophet, peace be upon him, with a rotten bone in his hand and said, "Muhammad says, 'No doubt, Allah will resurrect the dead.' I swear on Lat and Uzza that I will go to him and win by arguing!

"Oh, Muhammad! So, you say that after rotting, Allah will resurrect this bone again, right?"

The Prophet said, "Yes! This is what I am saying!"

Ubayy ibn Khalaf made a mocking face and said, "So you think that Allah will resurrect this after it rots, ha?"

He crumbled the bone in his hand and while scattering it towards the Prophet he said, "Oh, Muhammad! Who will resurrect this after it rots? Are we supposedly going to be

turned to how we were after we turn into this rotten bone? Who is the one that will resurrect us after we turn into this?"

The Prophet said, "Yes, Allah will kill you! Then resurrect you; and then, He will put you in Hell!"

With that, Allah revealed these verses of the Qur'an to the Prophet, peace be upon him:

Can man not see that We created him from a drop of fluid? Yet– lo and behold!– he disputes openly, producing arguments against Us, forgetting his own creation. He says, 'Who can give life back to bones after they have decayed?' Say, 'He who created them in the first place will give them life again: He has full knowledge of every act of creation.

Surah Ya Sin 36:77–79

When the trumpet is blown

Now you're wondering what will happen when Allah wants to bring us all back to life. You want such an example that you can say, "Aha! Now it makes sense!" so that your mind can understand it more clearly.

As you know when one of Allah's greatest angels, Israfel, blows the trumpet, given the name Sur, Qiyamah the Day of Resurrection will begin.

When the Trumpet is sounded a single time, when the earth and its mountains are raised high and then crushed with a single blow, on that Day the Great Event will come to pass. The sky will be torn apart on that Day, it will be so frail.
Surah Al-Haqqah 69:13–16

The second time the trumpet is blown, all dead people will be resurrected. This will happen in an instant.

The Trumpet will be sounded and— lo and behold!— they will rush out to their Lord from their graves.

Surah Ya Sin 36:51

So far we have seen how all bodies will be recreated one by one from both the Qur'an and the Prophet's example of the dead, dry earth coming to life in spring. But what's niggling your mind is how all these people's souls that have lived on this earth since our father Adam, are going to be returned to their body at once.

That is, how this will happen in an instant as soon as the trumpet is blown.

Here is an example for you.

There was an army. The army was made up of thousands of soldiers. After training all day, the general ordered the army's trumpeter to blow his trumpet and sound the order for the soldiers to disperse and take a rest.

All the soldiers ran here and there, some lay down under a tree, others went to play games.

After some time, the army's general gave another order to the trumpeter. This time to blow the sound for the soldiers to come back.

All those soldiers who heard the sound of that trumpet obeyed unquestioningly and came together.

So like this, when the time for resurrection comes, our Lord orders Israfel to blow the trumpet. When the trumpet is blown, all souls will pay attention to this sound.

Everyone will go into his or her own body. No one will be indifferent to this sound...

Because the order would have come from Allah.

If a general, who is an ordinary person, can gather all his soldiers with the sound of a trumpet, of course Allah, the Creator of the universe, can summon all people He created from the beginning of mankind up to this day with a trumpet's sound.

Souls return to their bodies and they find life in an instance; this is illustrated in this way:

Think of a city, a great city where millions of lights are switched on all at once.

All of this city's electricity may be controlled from one centre. If you turn off one switch in that centre, all the lights in the city will turn off. If you turn it on, they will all be lit. All those millions of lights will switch on at the same time. If we want, we could cover all the cities of the world, or even cover the whole Earth with lights, and turn them on or off from one centre. In an instance, with one move.

If electricity, which Allah has created and given to our service, is like this, of course with His one order billions of bodies will resurrect and find life again.

In an instance as well.

Why do we need to know Allah's names?

God—there is no god but Him—the most
excellent names belong to Him.
Surah Ta Ha 20:8

IMAGINE YOU HAD a friend called Mahir. He
is a skilful GARDENER who grows all kinds
of flowers in his garden. But Mahir's skills
aren't limited to gardening.

Mahir is also a very good CARPENTER at
the same time. He can make various tables and
chairs from timber and wood in his workshop.

Mahir is also a great COOK! The fame of
his delicious food has spread throughout the
whole city.

Let's imagine that Mahir is also an ARTIST.

Because of all of his skills, Mahir is called all of these names:

GARDENER
CARPENTER
COOK
ARTIST

Because of your friend's numerous qualities, his name "Mahir" would mean that much more to you.

You would know that "Mahir" is a gardener, a carpenter, a cook and an artist at the same time.

If you need help planting a flower, you wouldn't go to anyone else; you'd go straight to Mahir, the gardener.

If you need a chair, you would ask Mahir, the carpenter.

When you need a recipe, you know that Mahir, the cook, will offer you the best one.

If you need a painting to hang on a wall in your house, again, you would knock on Mahir's door, as he is an artist.

If you weren't aware of Mahir's various skills and separate names, the name "Mahir!" wouldn't mean much to you.

If somebody asked, "Who is Mahir?"

You would say, "You know, our Mahir!"

You wouldn't be able to mention that he's a gardener, or the tables and chairs he makes...

You wouldn't have anything to say about the delicious food he makes, or about his artistic pictures.

"Mahir?" you'd say, "Yes, I know him. How could I not know him? You know, he's Mahir..."

Just like this, when we say, "Allah" it's only possible to know who we are praying to, begging and taking refuge in, by knowing Allah's names and powers.

Otherwise, when we are asked, "Who is Allah?" we can only answer like, "Allah! Is there anyone that doesn't know Allah?"

We must get to know Allah.

We must try to learn His beautiful names and the meanings of His beautiful names.

What kind of an excuse can we have to not study and fail this test when we have a teacher like the Prophet, peace be upon him, a text book like the Holy Qur'an, and such a spectacular school, the Earth, situated in a universe with countless signs of Allah and His beautiful names?

Allah's beautiful names

First you must know this: Allah's beautiful names, in other words Asma al-Husnâ, are not like the ones on our birth certificates.

Because what you call "my name" is not exactly true. They are names given to us by our parents when we were born.

In high school, I had this teacher. Her name was Filiz, which means sprout in Turkish She was a very small woman. From time to time, she would moan about her height and say, "They called me Filiz but I've stopped growing upwards like a plant!"

She would laugh and make us all laugh as well.

One of my friends was called Mülayim. Mülayim means mild-mannered, and as gentle as a dove, in Turkish. Yet our Mülayim was definitely not gentle. Wherever there was a fight Mülayim was there. But if you asked, he would say, "My name is Mülayim!"

There was also Haşmet, which means majesty in Turkish. But he had no grandness about him. He was a tiny, quiet child with a waxy complexion.

Poor Haşmet, he was continually knocked about by Mülayim!

If they both truly owned their name, it would be impossible for Mülayim to knock

Haşmet about!

To be a true owner of a name, you must be like it. You must embody the characteristics of that name.

If Haşmet was a man of real importance; and Mülayim was as delicate and calm as a butterfly, then we could say these names really belonged to them.

You get the names that really belong to you according to what you do in your life in the years to come, how you live and what kind of a person you are.

For example if you write, they will give you the name WRITER.

If you paint, one of your names would be ARTIST.

The things you do show whether you're a writer or an artist.

Those who see your writing call you writer, and those who see your paintings call you artist. Those that look more closely can understand what kind of a writer or artist you are as well. The skill of you being a writer or artist is seen through your actions.

Even if people don't see you, they'll know you're a WRITER or an ARTIST by examining your work. They might not know whether you're tall or short, the colour of your hair and eyes, or the shape of your face, but they can learn a lot about what kind of a writer or artist you are.

Apart from this, as some of the features of your character begin to show over time, this will also become a name for you.

For example, if you are someone that likes to give presents to those around you, someone who really enjoys helping the poor and meeting the needs of the needy, those who see you doing this will give you the name GENEROUS.

If you're a very compassionate person your name will be KIND; if you're very intelligent you'll be WISE.

If you're a trustworthy person, they will call you RELIABLE.

All these names and attributes won't be on

your birth certificate. But they will belong to you and they will describe you.

Now coming back to our point, our little minds can of course never understand Allah.

When we are so far from understanding the vast universe He created, of course we won't understand Allah who created all of this from nothing.

We can only look at the creation of Allah to understand Him.

We can learn many things about Allah by looking at the universe as if it were the books of a writer, and examining the skies and the Earth as if they were an artist's paintings.

Everything Allah includes in the universe book, whether it is a star, atoms, the Sun or ants, shows us something about Him and helps us to understand His names.

For example, Allah, who shows mercy to all beings He created, is AR-RAHMAN, the Compassionate. He shows His compassion by putting sweet milk in the breasts of all mothers on Earth.

Allah who's eternally far from all bad things is
AL-QUDDUS, the Pure One. From bird's wings
to trees' leaves, He creates everything pure.

Allah who places stars, moons, suns and
planets in the depths of space is able to do
anything.

The eternal greatness of space shows the
infinity of His greatness and might to all those
who lift their heads and look up.

By seeing these wonders we understand Allah
is AL-QADIR, the Powerful, and
AL-MUTAKABBIR, the Greatest.

Allah who creates everything from
nonexistence is AL-KHALIQ, the Creator.
Whatever there is, it is there because He said,
"Be!"

Allah who created the fruits, flowers and
insects in perfect harmony is AL-BARI, the
Maker of Order.

On the hand-sized faces of all the people
on Earth, Allah's name, who created each one
different from another, shows that he is
AL-MUSAWWIR, the Shaper of Beauty.

Allah, who blesses us with everything in our lives, from parents to presents, is AL-WAHHAB, the Giver of All.

Allah who created a planet of plenty, with enough to fulfill the needs of every mouth and stomach he created, is AR-RAZZAQ, the Sustainer.

Allah who opens up seeds sleeping under soil during spring is AL-FATTAH, the Opener.

Allah who gives us the blessing of hearing is of course One who hears. AS-SAMIH, the

All-Hearing, is one of His beautiful names.

Allah who gives us the blessing of sight is One who sees everything, whether what He sees is in light or darkness, whether big or small. He is AL-BASIR, the All-Seeing.

Seeds that sleep under the soil for months, sometimes years and even centuries, and then sprout and grow, show Allah is AL-HAFIZ, the Preserver.

Allah, who gives rain to seeds and milk to babies, knows everyone's needs and makes it available to them. One of His beautiful names is AL-MUQIT, the Nourisher.

Another one of Allah's names is AR-RAQIB, the Watchful, as He who is closer to us than our jugular vein. He is closer to us than everything and everyone.

And we love Allah more than everyone and everything.

Allah is AL-WADUD, the Loving One. He is the One most deserving of being loved.

Allah is AL-WALI, the Protector, who is always a friend and helper to His good

servants.

From stars to tree leaves, from a canary's feather to every droplet of rain, He who knows the details of everything He created is AL-MUHSI, the Reckoner, the Appraiser.

How many flower buds sprout every year, how many daisies shoot up amongst grass every spring, how many babies smile at their mother every minute? Allah knows the number of all these things because He creates all of it and possesses the knowledge of it all.

He is AL-MUHYI, the One who fills the Earth with life. Life belongs to Him and only He can give life.

And Allah has countless other beautiful

names like these. When we learn these names we'll know well what kind of a God we pray to, seek refuge in and beg when we say, "Allah! My Lord!"

When we get hungry we ask Him for our livelihood; when we get ill we ask Him for recovery; when we are scared we seek refuge in Him; when we get into trouble we call to Him. We continue to knock on His door for our countless needs.

He, with His endless beautiful names, is the One who wrapped us with one thousand and one blessings and created us from nothing.

We know both that death comes from Him and so does resurrection and new life.

He is the one that everything needs but He needs nothing!

We love Him more than everyone and we know that He loves us more than everyone.

We wait for both spring from Him and Heaven as well.

We don't knock on any other door; we don't hold our hands out to anything else.

We seek refuge in Him and hold onto
His compassion with all our faults, all our
mistakes, all our poverty, all our weakness.

He is our Lord!

He is the One whose compassion embraces
all!

And He is the One who likes to forgive!

About the author

ÖZKAN ÖZE was born in Turkey in 1974. While at high school, he started working at Zafer Magazine's editorial office in Istanbul and discovered his love of literature and books. Since then he has gone on to become the editor of Zafer Publications Group and continually writes. He is married with two children.

Özkan wrote the "I Wonder About Islam" series because he believes that questions are prayers. Asking one is like saying, "Teach me to understand." They act as keys that lead us through doors to new worlds that are more interesting and beautiful than we thought possible.

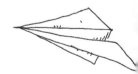

The "I Wonder About Islam" series

The "I Wonder About Islam" series give young readers answers to the BIG questions they have about Islam in brilliant little books. Written in a friendly and accessible style for today's youth, these are essential companions for questioning young minds.

Books in the "I Wonder About Islam" series: